RL 3.3

D060179G

A SMOOTH MOVE

Story by **Berniece Rabe**

Pictures by **Linda Shute**

Albert Whitman & Company   Niles, Illinois

Library of Congress Cataloging-in-Publication Data

Rabe, Berniece.
    A smooth move.

    Summary: When his family moves from Oregon to
Washington, D.C., Gus decides to record their
experiences and his own feelings in a journal.
    [1. Moving, Household—Fiction]   I. Shute, Linda,
ill. II. Title.
PZ7.R105Sm 1987   [E]   87-2099
ISBN 0-8075-7486-4

7/98 J fund 13⁰⁰

Text © 1987 by Berniece Rabe
Illustrations © 1987 by Linda McElhiney Shute
Published in 1987 by Albert Whitman & Company
Published simultaneously in Canada
by General Publishing, Limited, Toronto
10   9   8   7   6   5   4   3   2   1

For Chad Rabe B.R.

For all the kids who have moved
to Fairfax County, Virginia L.S.

March 25
I am Gus, and this is my journal.
For a long time, I've lived with my mom,
my dad, my little brother, Lee, and my cat, Ki-Ki,
in a long, low house near Portland, Oregon.
Now my dad has a new job in Washington, D.C.,
and we have to move. I'm not sure I like that.
I know I'll miss my friends.
But I have to be brave.
Mom said keeping a journal might help.

April 2
Dad's already moved to Washington, D.C.,
to start his job. We talk to him on the phone,
and today we got a letter. He says he misses us . . .

He sent pictures of our new, tall house.
My bedroom will be on the third floor.
That sounds neat! Most of the time,
I want to go to Washington, D.C.
I miss my dad very much.

April 13
Our house finally sold! Mom is very happy.
Some strangers with three kids bought it.
The biggest girl will get my bedroom.
Dad laughed on the telephone.
He said, "Hey, Gus, that came off smooth!
Wait until you see your new, tall school—
it's standing up on end!"
I tried to laugh, too. I really do like to laugh.
But I don't know if I'll like a tall school.

April 14
Today my good friends Thad and Jane and Paul
walked with me for the last time to my long, low school.
I was sad, but Paul told me a joke I hadn't heard:
"Where do penguins keep their money?
In a snow bank!" That made me laugh.

My teacher gave me my report card
to take to my new school.
It was a great report card, except for one line:
"Gus is a good student, but he is a talker."
I sure didn't feel like laughing when I read *that*.
This move won't be so smooth
when my new teacher finds out I'm a talker!

April 15

I dreamed that I went all alone to the new school.
The teacher read my report card out loud.
Everyone laughed. I felt awful.
I don't like strangers laughing at me.
I was glad to wake up still in Portland.
But the sign in our front yard says "Sold,"
so we have to move.
Mom gave me a list of things to do:

1. Put clothes you will need right away
   into your big suitcase.
2. Pack two favorite toys.
3. Pack two favorite books.
4. Put toys into toy box.

I added:

5. Get friends' addresses.
6. Take journal on plane.

April 16
Men came to pack our things into big boxes.
That did not go smooth. They came too early!
While Mom was in Lee's room changing his diaper,
they packed the leftover bread dough she was going to bake!

I said, "Hey, you'd better not do that!"
They didn't pay any attention to me.
Then they packed dirty dishes from the sink
and clothes from the washer—still dripping wet!
I laughed when I told Mom, but she didn't laugh.

All the furniture and all the boxes
went into a big moving van.
We waved goodbye to the men as they drove away.

Mom sighed as she looked at the messy floors.
"Things could be worse," I said.
"The bread dough could rise and rise and rise
until all our toys and furniture are covered.
I know it could happen. I know all about yeast."
Mom said, "Gus, don't be such a worrier.
Go and get ready for the slumber party tonight."

April 17
Slumber parties are great!
Thad and Jane and Paul brought hot chocolate,
black licorice strings, nacho chips,
flashlights, and sleeping bags.
Mom's friends came with pizza, cans of pop,
a broom, and some toilet paper.
Everyone stayed to sleep over in our empty house.
It seemed strange and spooky with no furniture.
My friends and I told jokes all night long.

But in the morning we had to say goodbye
to our long, low house and our friends.
Mom cried. I did, too, and so did Lee.
Ki-Ki meowed in her travel carrier.

Thad and his mom took us to the airport.
They promised to write. We promised to write back.
We all waved and waved.

April 17 (written on an airplane)
When we took off, I could see Mt. St. Helens and Mt. Hood.
Now I can just see clouds. We're really high—flying
from the west coast of the United States of America
to the east coast of the United States of America.
Ki-Ki is in her cat carrier under Mom's seat.
I told the flight attendant about Ki-Ki and about
our old house and our new house and all about yeast.

So far, I've played word games with Mom
and tickled Lee in the ribs.
And I've talked to other passengers.
We ate lunch from a tray on the seat back.
Smooth going. Well, not quite.
I'll have to stop writing now.
Ki-Ki is howling. She wants to get out.

Still April 17 (still in airplane)
I put my hand inside the carrier
and talked soft and sweet to Ki-Ki till she purred.
The captain announced, "We're now crossing
the Mississippi River. Visibility is good."
I looked out the window and saw
a wide river and some very flat country.

Mom showed me a big map in the airline magazine.
I found the Mississippi River on it.
"We've flown right over the moving van," Mom said.
"It had a headstart, but we'll beat it to the east coast.
We'll live in a hotel for three days
until the van comes with our furniture."

Late on April 17
At five o'clock, Dad met us at the gate.
I hugged him hard. Then I told him, "Your watch is wrong.
We left Portland more than six hours ago. It's two o'clock."
Dad explained to me about time zones.
It's three hours later on the east coast than on the west coast.
That's because the earth is turning away from the sun.
I really like being with Dad again.

And the hotel is great! It has a pool and a game room.
My brother has a crib, my parents have one king-sized bed,
and I get the other king-sized bed all to myself.
Ki-Ki's bed is under my bed, and she's been growling a lot.
I said, "Give her tuna. She never growls if she has tuna.
Dry cat food is for the birds!"
"Well, hardly," Dad said, but he fed Ki-Ki tuna. She purred.

April 20

It's been three days, and the moving van hasn't come.
We keep feeding Ki-Ki more and more tuna. It smells.
Mom said she's tired of the hotel, but I like it.
I ride up and down the elevator with Ki-Ki and talk to people.
I get soda pop and peanuts from the machines.
We all swim in the pool and play in the game room.

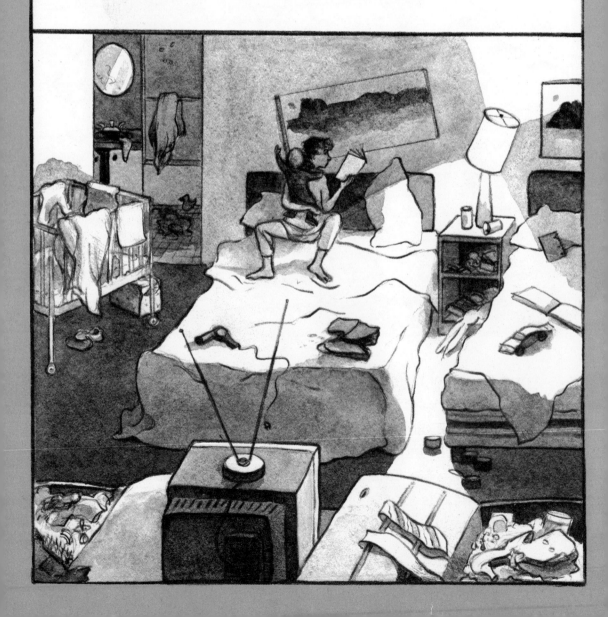

April 22
Today we got bad news.
The moving van is stalled in Utah.
It won't come for another week.
I wonder if the bread dough rose until it covered
the engine?
Mom gave a deep sigh. Lee pulled Ki-Ki's tail.
"Let's all try to be patient and happy," Dad said.

So I rode the elevator one hundred times today.
I told lots of people about the bread dough
and how it had probably covered all our furniture.
They all thought that was pretty funny.
I laughed, too.
Dad said he likes to hear me laugh.
Mom said I was being a good sport and making
this difficult move go as smooth as possible.

April 24
We still sleep nights at the hotel.
But during the days, we explore our new house.
Dad was right—it is tall! There are lots of stairs.
I like my new room up in the treetops.
Ki-Ki hid from us. I was the one who found her.
That's how I learned all the hiding places.

April 26
We went to see my new school today.
It's very tall, too, with three fire escapes.
I'd like to climb all three, but I won't.
There are lots of kids on the playground.
I said, "I might not like it. I don't know anyone here."
"A talker like you, Gus?" Dad said.
"You won't have trouble making friends."
He may be right.
But what if my new teacher doesn't like talkers?

April 29
The big moving van made it at last!
Joseph, a boy my age, came to watch.
I told him all about the rising bread dough.
He thought it was pretty funny, and
he could hardly wait to see it.

Well, the dishes were crusted over.
And Ki-Ki's nose did a lot of twitching
when she went near the dirty laundry.
The yeast dough was hard as a rock. It hadn't risen at all.
The temperature wasn't warm enough.
I learned some more about yeast.
"What made this van stall in Utah?" I asked the driver.
"A mud slide blocked the road," he told me.

Mom dashed out with money for ice cream bars for me
and my new friend, if I promised not to bother the men.
I promised, and everything got unloaded.
So moving-in day went smooth as ice cream.

May 2
I rode to school today with Joseph, on a yellow bus.
But I didn't tell him any jokes. I didn't say much at all.
I just held onto my report card that says I am a talker.
I held onto it inside my shirt.

My new teacher is short—a short teacher in a tall school!
That's pretty funny, and I told her so.
She smiles just like my old teacher.
So I told her about the bread dough. She laughed.

She took me to the media center,
and I found two of my favorite books there. Then she said,
"I'll look at your report card while you check out your books."
She held out her hand.

I hoped she'd forgotten about it. I pulled out my
report card from under my shirt and held my breath.

"Um-m-m," she said, "I do enjoy a good talker.
Talkers make good storytellers." She smiled at me.
Then I laughed. I mean I *really* laughed!
Everything was smooth sailing after that.

Still May 2
Going home on the bus today,
I asked Joseph and some other kids,
"Where do penguins keep their money?"
No one knew, so I said, "In a snow bank!"
They laughed. Then they told me some jokes I hadn't
heard before, and we all sang some pretty silly songs.

But later, I got to missing my old friends.
I wished I could show them my new house and tall school.
Our family went out for pizza again, same as last night.
It's a terrific pizza place we've found. I love pizza.
I wish my old friends could see this new pizza place.

May 8

Today Dad took us to see the White House
and the pandas at the National Zoo.
Living in Washington, D.C., is neat!

May 10

This will be the last page in my moving journal.
I'll write a whole page letter to my Portland friends.
I know just what I'll say. I'll say,

Dear Thad, Jane, and Paul,
   Our whole move went real smooth.
   We have a big, beautiful country.
   I know. I flew over all of it.
   Come visit Washington, D.C.
   I'll take you to see where the President of
   the entire United States of America lives.
   Come see my new, tall house and meet
   my new friends. Heard any new jokes?
   Write back real soon. I miss you.
   But I think I'm going to like it here.

                                    GUS